D0950946

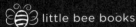 little bee books

New York, NY

For more information about special discounts on bulk purchases, please contact Little Bee Books at sales@littlebeebooks.com.

Library of Congress Cataloging-in-Publication Data
Names: Newton, A. I., author. | Sarkar, Anjan, illustrator.
Title: The new kid / by A. I. Newton; illustrated by Anjan Sarkar.
Description: First edition. | New York, NY: Little Bee Books, [2018] | Series: The alien next door; #1 | Summary: While his scientist-parents study Earth, second-grader Zeke tries to fit in but Harris, a classmate, notices his abilities and sets out to prove Zeke is an alien. | Identifiers: LCCN 2017003461 | Subjects: | CYAC: Extraterrestrial beings—Fiction. | Ability—Fiction. | Friendship—Fiction. | Schools—Fiction. | Classification: LCC PZ7.1.N498 New 2018 | DDC [Fic]—dc23
LC record available at https://lccn.loc.gov/2017003461

Printed in China RRD 1020
ISBN 978-1-4998-0559-8 (hardcover)
First Edition 10 9 8 7 6 5 4 3 2
ISBN 978-1-4998-0558-1 (paperback)
First Edition 10 9 8
ISBN 978-1-4998-0560-4 (ebook)

littlebeebooks.com

THE ALIEN NEXT DOOR

THE NEW KID

by A. I. Newton
illustrated by Anjan Sarkar

little bee books

TABLE OF CONTENTS

THE NEW SCHOOL

THE NEW KID SAT ALONE IN the back of the bus. He was on his way to his first day at a new school.

Once again.

He watched as the other kids fooled around. They giggled and yelled. No one else seemed to be just sitting in their seat.

Except him. The new kid.

Once again.

Taking this "bus" thing to school with everyone else is really dumb, he thought. *Back home we got to school on our own. And much faster than in this clunky yellow hunk of metal. And instead of messing around the whole way like these kids, we had time to think and prepare for learning. But this . . .*

The new kid shook his head. No one on the bus seemed to even notice that he was there.

Here we go again, he thought. *Will anyone like me? Will I make any friends? Why do my parents have to move so much?*

The new boy sighed. He knew why they were always moving. They were research scientists. Their work took them from place to place. And every time they moved, he had to start over in a new school. He had to make new friends. He had to learn how things were done in a new place.

"Hey, Charlie!" one kid shouted at his friend. "Did you finish last week's homework?"

"I finished it this morning," another kid shouted back. "Right on time!"

The bus rocked with laughter.

The new kid didn't understand.

What was funny about waiting until the last minute to do your schoolwork? He didn't like always feeling different. He was tired of being the strange new kid once again.

And he missed his home.

I have friends back home. I know how stuff works there. All of this is so . . . different, so strange.

The bus slowed to a stop and the doors opened. The kids bounded down the stairs and ran toward the school.

The new kid got out of his seat. He walked slowly to the front of the bus to exit.

"Good luck today," said the bus driver. She smiled warmly at him. It made him feel a little better.

Here I go again, he thought. Then he took a deep breath, walked into the school, and hoped for the best.

2
THE NEW KID

HARRIS WALKER LOOKED around his second-grade classroom. He leaned over to his best friend, Roxy Martinez.

"I heard that a new boy is joining our class," said Harris. "He moved in next door to me yesterday."

"Really?" asked Roxy. "Where's he from?"

"Some place called Tragas," Harris replied. "I tried to look it up online. It's not even on a map!"

Their teacher, Ms. Graham, walked into the classroom.

"Good morning, class," she said. "We have a new student joining us today."

Harris whispered in Roxy's ear, "See, I told you!"

"Harris, is there a problem?" asked Ms. Graham.

"No, Ms. Graham," Harris said sheepishly.

"Well then, please pay attention. The new boy's name is Zeke. I want the entire class to make him feel welcome."

A whistling sound came from outside the classroom door.

Ms. Graham walked over and opened the door. A short boy with dark hair stood in the hall. Harris could see that he was wearing thick, black-rimmed glasses.

"You must be Zeke," said Ms. Graham.

"I am," replied the boy.

"Well, please come in," Ms. Graham said. "Why did you whistle at the door? Why didn't you just knock?"

Zeke looked confused. "Where I come from, that's how we ask permission to come into a room," he explained. Then he took a seat at an empty desk.

"Weird, huh?" Harris whispered to Roxy.

"I think it's kind of interesting," she whispered back.

Ms. Graham started writing on the board.

"Please write this homework assignment in your notebook or tablet," she said.

Ms. Graham, noticing Zeke, looked puzzled.

"Are you all right, Zeke?" she asked.

The new boy's eyes were shut tight. His fingertips were pressed against the sides of his head.

Zeke opened his eyes.

"Yes, Ms. Graham. I'm fine," he said. "I was just writing down the assignment."

Zeke held up his tablet. The assignment was there, all typed out.

"How did he do that?" Harris whispered to Roxy.

"Maybe he has a wireless keyboard under his desk," Roxy replied.

"But his hands were—"

"Harris, do you have a question?" asked Ms. Graham.

"No, Ms. Graham," he said, looking down.

At lunch that day, Harris and Roxy sat together as usual. Zeke sat by himself.

"I feel bad for Zeke," said Roxy. "He doesn't know anyone. I'm going to ask him to sit with us."

"Why?" Harris asked. "We don't even know him!"

"But he's your neighbor, and this is our chance to get to know him," Roxy replied. Then she called out to Zeke, "Zeke, why don't you come eat lunch with us?"

Zeke picked up a round metal ball with blinking lights he had on the table in front of him and joined Harris and Roxy where they were sitting.

"What's that?" Harris asked.

"My lunch container," Zeke explained.

"Odd-looking lunch box," Harris mumbled.

"So how do you like Jefferson Elementary School so far?" Roxy asked.

"It is . . . different," said Zeke.

Zeke opened his blinking metal lunch box and pulled out a large green ball. Pink strings dangled from the ball. He shoved the whole thing into his mouth. His cheeks puffed out. He looked like he was eating two softballs at the same time.

Without moving his mouth at all, Zeke's cheeks slowly got smaller and smaller.

"What are you eating?" asked Harris.

"It's called a dweelop," Zeke explained. "It's a fruit that grows all over Tragas, where I come from."

"But you didn't even chew it," Harris said.

"It's pretty soft," Zeke replied.

A few minutes later, the bell sounded. Lunchtime was over. Harris cleared his tray and headed back to class.

This new kid is definitely weird! he thought.

3 ZEKE AT HOME

AFTER SCHOOL WAS OVER, Zeke walked back to his new house, opening the front door. He had just finished his first day at a new school. He was happy to be home.

"How was your first day, Zekelabraxis?" asked a voice from across the living room.

Zeke looked over and saw a creature with green skin. It had five eyes, and six tentacles extending from its shoulders.

"Xad! I thought we were going to use Earth names and bodies. . . ." Zeke whined.

"You are indeed correct, Zeke," said Xad.

The green being began to glow. When the glowing stopped, a human-looking man stood in its place. He was short with black hair. He wore the same thick, black-rimmed glasses that Zeke wore.

Zeke's mom joined them.

"Brezkat plitnob, Zekelabraxis?" she said. She floated into the room, two feet off the ground. She, too, had green skin, and she had seven eyes and four tentacles.

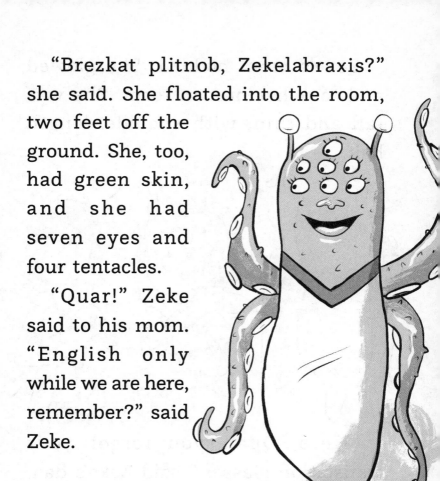

"Quar!" Zeke said to his mom. "English only while we are here, remember?" said Zeke.

Zeke's mom nodded. She glowed and took her human form. She was tall and thin, with shoulder-length hair.

"Here, Quar, you forgot your translation glasses," said Zeke's dad. He handed his wife a pair of thick, black-rimmed glasses. She slipped them on.

Zeke thought about the translation glasses. And how, by smoothly translating the language of Tragas into the language of whatever planet they were on, they allowed his parents to do their research and allowed him to go to school.

"So, how was your first day, Zeke?" Quar repeated her question. This time, it was translated into English.

"They have very strange customs on this planet," said Zeke. "It is not like Tragas. They don't absorb their food through their cheeks. They chew it with something called 'teeth.' And they can't mind-project to write."

"Speaking of writing," said Zeke's mom, "do you have any missions from school?"

"On Earth they call it 'homework,'" Zeke explained. "And yes, I do."

Zeke read the assignment on his tablet. Then he pressed a button on the table next to him. A large screen appeared just above his head.

Zeke pressed his fingertips against the sides of his head. He shut his eyes tightly and thought about the answers to his homework questions. Numbers appeared on the giant screen.

To Zeke, he was just doing his homework—the same way he did it on his home planet of Tragas.

$$49 + 82 = 131$$
$$6 \times 12 =$$

4
ALIENS!

THAT SAME DAY AFTER school, Harris sat at the desk in his room. He was trying to do his homework. But all he could think about was the strange new kid in his class. He decided to call Roxy.

"What did you think of that new kid, Zeke?" Harris asked when Roxy picked up the phone.

"He was nice," she replied.

"He was weird," said Harris.

"Just because someone is different doesn't mean they're weird," Roxy pointed out.

Harris thought about that for a moment. He wasn't sure what to think of Zeke.

"I know, but still, I think there's something off about him. Anyway, I have to finish my homework," Harris said. "See ya tomorrow."

When his homework was done, Harris opened the latest issue of his favorite comic book, *Tales from Alien Worlds!* He flopped onto his bed and opened it. He saw alien spaceships zooming through the air. They passed tall orange towers that glowed.

What a cool alien world this is! Harris thought.

He flipped the page. There was a picture of an alien with his eyes shut tight. The alien's fingertips pressed against his head. In front of the alien, words appeared on a giant screen.

That's how Zeke wrote on his tablet! This is too weird.

Harris finished the comic. He looked out the window at Zeke's house. *Why is it always dark over there?*

He got ready for bed, but couldn't stop thinking about Zeke.

The next day at school, Harris found Roxy at recess. She had a soccer ball at her feet. Roxy and Harris were both on the Jefferson Elementary School soccer team.

"Let's practice," she said.

Roxy kicked the ball across the playground. Harris chased it down and kicked it back.

Roxy's next kick rolled right past Harris. Instead of paying attention to the ball, he was staring at the swing set.

"Do you see that?" Harris asked, pointing.

Roxy looked and saw Zeke balanced on a swing on just one finger. His body stood upside down, straight as an arrow. She and Harris ran over to him.

"What the heck are you doing?" Harris asked.

Zeke looked at them.

I can't tell them the truth, Zeke thought. *That this exercise helps me mind-project more clearly.*

"I am planning on trying out for the gymnastics team," Zeke said. "I was good at gymnastics in Tragas."

Harris had his doubts. But before he could say anything else, the bell rang. Recess was over. Harris and Roxy hurried back into the school.

That evening after dinner, Harris joined his dad in front of the TV. It was time for the Monster Movie of the Week. Harris and his dad never missed it.

"This should be a good one," said Harris's dad. "It's called *Monster Aliens from Planet Z.*"

The movie began. A giant alien spaceship landed right in the middle of a park. People ran in panic.

The spaceship's door slid open. An alien walked out. Only, the alien didn't walk on its feet. It walked upside down on its fingertips.

Just like Zeke! Harris thought. *That's it! That explains everything. My new neighbor is definitely an alien!*

5 SCIENCE LAB

THE NEXT DAY AT SCHOOL, Zeke felt bored.

Well, that didn't take long, he thought. *I always get so worried about starting a new school, but in this place, everything they do is so simple. If I can't be home, I wish I were back on Charbock.*

Charbock was the last planet Zeke's family had researched.

At least there, kids could do cool stuff like teleport from place to place. And control the weather with their minds. It was a very interesting planet. Not like Earth, Zeke thought as he entered the science lab.

"Okay, class, today's experiment is all about colors," said Mr. Mills, the science teacher. "We are going to combine certain colors to create other colors. In front of you are red, green, yellow, and blue solutions. Experiment and see how combining the colors changes them into new ones."

Zeke combined yellow and blue to make green. He combined blue and red to make purple. Then he mixed red and yellow to make orange. He was the first one in the class to finish.

Zeke glanced over at Harris and Roxy. They were still combining colors, but Harris was also staring at him.

Why does Harris keep staring at me like that? Zeke wondered. *Could he actually suspect that I'm not from this planet?*

As the other kids worked with the basic colors, Zeke got an idea.

This could be fun, he thought.

He combined all the solutions in one glass beaker. Then he grabbed the beaker with both hands. He sent vibrations from his hands into the glass and the colors inside the beaker started to swirl.

A few seconds later, Zeke had created a twirling rainbow right inside his beaker.

He glanced toward Roxy and Harris.

Roxy saw the rainbow and smiled. "Wow, that is *so* cool!"

But Harris's eyes opened wide.

"How did you do that, Zeke?" asked Harris. "That's impossible!"

"What's impossible?" asked Mr. Mills. He walked over to Zeke's table and saw the rainbow spinning in his beaker.

"Actually, Harris, it is not impossible," said Mr. Mills. "There is a chemical you can add to your colors that will make that happen."

Harris frowned. Then Mr. Mills turned to Zeke.

"However, Zeke, that chemical is kept in a drawer labeled DO NOT OPEN." Mr. Mills explained. "I admire your curiosity and inventiveness. But please do not open any drawers without permission, there are some dangerous things in there."

Zeke couldn't admit that he didn't use any chemicals, he just used his powers. He stayed quiet. His parents were very clear about revealing his powers to anyone on Earth.

"Unlike Charbock, Earth has not yet made contact with anyone outside of Earth," his father had said on their journey to their new planet. "You must never reveal your powers to anyone there."

The bell rang ending science lab.

As he left the room, Harris looked at Zeke and shook his head.

What if he finds out I'm an alien? Zeke thought. *I could ruin my parents' entire mission here.*

Zeke walked from the lab. *This is going to be a long school year,* he thought.

6
MOM AND DAD

AFTER SCHOOL, HARRIS AND Roxy walked home together.

"You know, I don't think you've been very welcoming to Zeke," said Roxy. "Just because he's different from you doesn't mean he isn't nice."

"I still think he's strange," Harris said.

"Well, I like him," said Roxy. "Is that why you *don't* like him? I can be friends with both of you, you know."

"That's not it," said Harris. "I've just seen him do some crazy stuff."

"And all of what you call 'crazy stuff' has a logical explanation," said Roxy. "I just think you're looking for reasons to not like Zeke."

Roxy turned onto her block. Harris kept walking.

He thought about what Roxy had said. Then he shrugged it off.

That evening at dinner, Harris's parents asked him about Zeke.

"How is that new boy doing?" asked his mom.

"I hope you are trying to make friends with him," added his dad.

"I don't know," said Harris. "He does all kinds of strange stuff. He even balanced on his fingertips, like the aliens in that movie, Dad."

"Harris, come on," said his dad. "You're too old to not know the difference between movies and real life."

"No, Dad, it's real!" Harris insisted. "I'm telling you the truth."

"Remember how much trouble you had making friends when you started at Jefferson until you met Roxy?" asked his mom. "I would hope that you would be extra nice to new kids who are trying to fit in."

"But, Mom, I—"

"I'm sure that if you take the time to get to know Zeke, you'll discover that he's just a normal kid like you," Mom said. "He might be different, but that's no reason not to be his friend."

Harris went to his room after dinner and started his homework. But again he had trouble concentrating.

Everyone is telling me that I'm wrong, but I know I'm not. I'm going to prove, once and for all, that Zeke is an alien!

THE NEXT DAY AT LUNCH,

Harris put his plan into motion. As he and Roxy walked into the cafeteria, Harris spotted Zeke.

"Hey, Zeke, why don't you sit with us for lunch?" he called out.

"Well, I'm glad you finally decided to be nice to him," said Roxy, smiling.

The three sat together at a table. Roxy pulled out a tunafish sandwich. Harris bit into his PB&J. Zeke took out a long purple string. He put one end into his mouth and slurped up the entire thing. Then he pulled out another one.

"What's that?" Harris asked in a very friendly voice.

"Gardash strands," said Zeke. "They are very popular in Tragas."

"Speaking of Tragas, where exactly is it?" Harris asked.

"South of here," replied Zeke.

"On this continent?" Harris asked.

"No," said Zeke, slurping down another gardash strand.

"So what's it next to?" asked Harris.

"Quarzinta," replied Zeke.

"I never heard of that either," said Harris.

"Someone doesn't know his geography," Zeke said.

Roxy giggled, and Harris looked down, embarrassed. His plan was going nowhere.

"So what's it like in Tragas?" asked Roxy.

"Well, there is bright yellow water in the lakes," said Zeke. "We have elevators that travel sideways, not up and down. And the snow is a glowing blue."

If that doesn't sound like an alien planet, I don't know what does! Harris thought.

"Sounds wonderful!" said Roxy. "So, I had an idea. Maybe we should all hang out this weekend. How about Saturday?"

Harris's eyes opened wide.

Hang out? he thought. *With an alien? That's too weird. But if I say no, Roxy will think I'm being mean.*

"I would like that, thank you," said Zeke.

"Why don't we all go to your house, Harris?" asked Roxy. "You have the biggest TV and some cool games. And wait till you meet his parents, Zeke. They're so nice!"

"Um . . . sure," said Harris. What else could he say?

Harris felt trapped.

Today is Thursday, he thought. *That only gives me one more day to prove that Zeke is an alien before I have to hang out with him—in my own house!*

8 MISSION: EARTH

THAT EVENING AT HOME, Zeke talked to his parents.

"I like some of the Earth stuff at school," he explained. "The bell that sounds between classes is the same tone as my meditation chime back on Tragas. It helps my mind-projection."

"Well that sounds nice," said Quar.

"I don't really like taking the school bus," said Zeke. "But the way the folding door opens is very clever."

"Have you met any nice Earth kids?" asked Xad.

"I think I have made a new friend," said Zeke. "Her name is Roxy. She has been very nice to me."

"That's wonderful, Zeke," said Quar.

"Oh, and Roxy and I have been invited to visit the home of the boy who lives next door, Harris, this weekend," said Zeke. "I'm a little worried about him. I think he may suspect that I'm what they would call an 'alien.'"

"Be careful, Zeke," said Xad. "You remember what I told you about Earth."

"I know," said Zeke. "I'm trying to fit in."

"Sounds to me like you're doing okay, Zeke," said Quar.

"But I still miss my friends on Tragas," said Zeke. "And it's Bonkas season there already. I'm going to have to miss another season watching my favorite team play."

"I know you miss it, Zeke," said Quar.

"It *is* the official sport of Tragas," Zeke said. "And no one on Earth has even heard of it!"

"Well, I have some good news for you," said Xad. "I've been adapting our long-range communications device to pick up broadcasts of Bonkas matches from Tragas. Maybe that will help you feel less homesick."

"Thanks, Xad!" said Zeke. "So, how long are you planning on staying on Earth?"

"It's hard to say, Zeke," said Xad. "It depends upon what my bosses want to learn about humans. Right now, we're assigned to study human clothing. Why do humans dress the way they do?"

"Why do boys and girls often dress so differently?" Quar continued. "Why do humans wear different clothing for work, play, fancy parties, and other things?"

A video appeared on the giant overhead screen where Zeke did his homework.

"This was our research at the giant group of stores today," said Xad.

"On Earth, they call this a 'mall,'" said Zeke.

The video showed a family with three children. Each kid held a different color shirt. They passed the shirts back and forth in front of a mirror.

"This one doesn't match my eyes," said one kid.

"This is the wrong color for my hair!" said another.

Zeke and his parents laughed. On Tragas, everyone wore the same style of clothing.

"Earth people can be pretty silly," said Zeke. "I can see why you'd want to study them."

9
PROOF AT LAST?

IT WAS ALREADY FRIDAY, and Harris was worried. Zeke would be coming to hang out at Harris's house the next day unless he was able to prove Zeke was an alien.

At recess, several grades were out on the playground together.

"I've got the soccer ball, Harris," said Roxy. "Ready?"

Roxy kicked the ball to him. Then she noticed Zeke standing all by himself.

"Hey, Zeke, do you want to play soccer with us?" she called out.

Zeke trotted over to Roxy.

"I don't know how to play soccer," he said.

"It's easy," Roxy said. "You kick the ball to another player or into the goal. And you can't touch the ball with your hands. Try it."

Zeke ran toward Harris.

"Harris, kick the ball to Zeke!" she shouted.

Harris kicked the ball right at Zeke.

Zeke stopped and got ready to kick it back. But when the ball reached him, it skipped over his foot.

To his amazement, Harris watched as Zeke just stood still and lifted one hand into the air. Zeke wiggled his hand. The soccer ball slowed down, stopped, then started rolling back toward Zeke.

Harris immediately turned to Roxy.

Did she just see that? Harris wondered. *That's proof that Zeke is an alien!*

But Roxy's back was to both boys just then. She had turned to talk to her friend, Samantha.

I can't believe that Roxy didn't see that, thought Harris. *I'm never going to prove this before tomorrow.*

Harris looked down and saw the ball speeding toward him. He kicked it to Zeke.

Again, Zeke missed the ball. It rolled toward the far corner of the playground. This time, Zeke chased after it.

When Zeke reached the ball, he saw a kindergartener crying under a basketball hoop.

"What's the matter?" asked Zeke, walking over to him.

The little boy pointed up at the hoop.

"My balloon slipped out of my hand and now it's stuck up there!" sobbed the boy.

Zeke looked up and saw the balloon stuck against the rim.

"I can get that for you," he said.

I'll bet you can, thought Harris. *You're probably going to fly up to the hoop, or transport the balloon down or something. You're going to do something weird, I know it! And this time, Roxy has to see it.*

"Roxy, look!" Harris called out. He pointed at Zeke.

This is it! Harris thought. *Roxy is finally going to see Zeke do something that will prove he's an alien!*

But when Roxy turned around, all she saw was a tall sixth grader from the basketball team leap up and grab the balloon's string. He handed it to the kindergartener.

Roxy rolled her eyes at Harris and shook her head.

Harris sighed. *I guess an alien is coming to my house after all!*

10 NEW FRIENDS

HARRIS WOKE UP SATURDAY

morning and was very nervous. Zeke was coming to his house today.

Around noon, both Roxy and Zeke arrived.

"Hi, Roxy, so nice to see you," said Harris's mom.

"Thanks for having us over, Mrs. Walker," said Roxy. "This is our new friend, Zeke."

"Welcome, Zeke," said Mrs. Walker.

"We've heard a whole lot about you from Harris," said Harris's dad.

"Thank you, Mr. Walker, Mrs. Walker," said Zeke. "I'm glad to be here."

"So," said Harris, "who wants to play some video games?"

Roxy raised her hand. Zeke looked at her and raised his as well.

The three friends sat down in front of the TV and each picked up a controller.

"This one is called *Cosmic Comet Blast*," said Harris. "The idea is to blast comets out of the sky before they crash into Earth. Ready . . . go!"

On the big screen, giant comets streaked across the sky.

"Fire your laser cannons!" shouted Harris.

Harris blasted a few comets. Roxy blew up a few more. Zeke wasn't doing much at first, but soon he destroyed every comet he aimed at.

"That was amazing, Zeke!" said Roxy.

"Yeah," said Harris. "Are you sure you never played this game before?"

"I'm sure, Harris," said Zeke. "They don't have video games in Tragas."

"No video games!" Harris said. "What do you do for fun?"

"We race in our zumda cycles," said Zeke. "We play Bonkas, which uses thin sticks and ten Bonkas balls. And we make up project-o-stories on our holo-screens."

"How come I've never heard of any of that stuff?" asked Harris skeptically.

"Oh, well, Tragas is very far away," explained Zeke.

"Who wants pizza?" Harris's mom called from the kitchen.

"What is pizza?" asked Zeke.

"Come on," said Harris. "You don't have pizza on Tragas? I thought everyone ate pizza." *That's definitely proof he's an alien!* thought Harris.

"I'm happy to try it," said Zeke.

Zeke, Roxy, Harris, and his parents sat around the kitchen table. They each grabbed a slice of pizza.

"I have never tasted anything like this," said Zeke. "I like it."

"Zeke, what do your parents do?" asked Mr. Walker.

"They are researchers," Zeke explained. "They move from place to place. That's why I move around so much. That's why I'm always starting over in a new school."

"That must be hard," said Mrs. Walker.

"I get used to it, I guess," Zeke said. "It helps when I make new friends." He smiled at Harris and Roxy.

"I know what I wanted to tell you, Zeke," said Roxy. "I'm trying out for the school play."

"Don't tell me that they don't have plays in Tragas," Harris said.

Zeke laughed. "No, we have plays in Tragas. In fact, I like to act. I have been in a few plays."

"Maybe you should try out, Zeke," said Roxy. "It's a great way to meet new kids."

"Thanks," said Zeke. "Maybe I will."

After lunch, the kids watched a movie—*Zombie Invasion from Beneath the Earth!*

"You have movies in Tragas, right?" asked Harris.

"Yes," replied Zeke. *Except ours are 4-D holo-projections. But I have to be careful what I tell Harris!* he thought to himself.

When the movie ended, it was time for Roxy and Zeke to go home.

"Thank you," said Zeke as he headed for the door. "I had a nice time."

"See you Monday," said Roxy.

"Well, Zeke seems like a very nice boy, Harris," said Mrs. Walker when Zeke and Roxy had gone. "All you had to do was give him a chance."

"I did have fun with Zeke today," Harris admitted.

But I still think he's an alien, Harris thought. *And one of these days I'm going to prove it!*

Zeke walked back over to his home next door.

"How was your visit, Zeke?" asked Xad.

"I had fun," Zeke said. "I think things might be okay here on Earth. I'm off to a good start. After all, I have already made two new friends!"

Read on for a sneak peek at the second book in the Alien Next Door series!

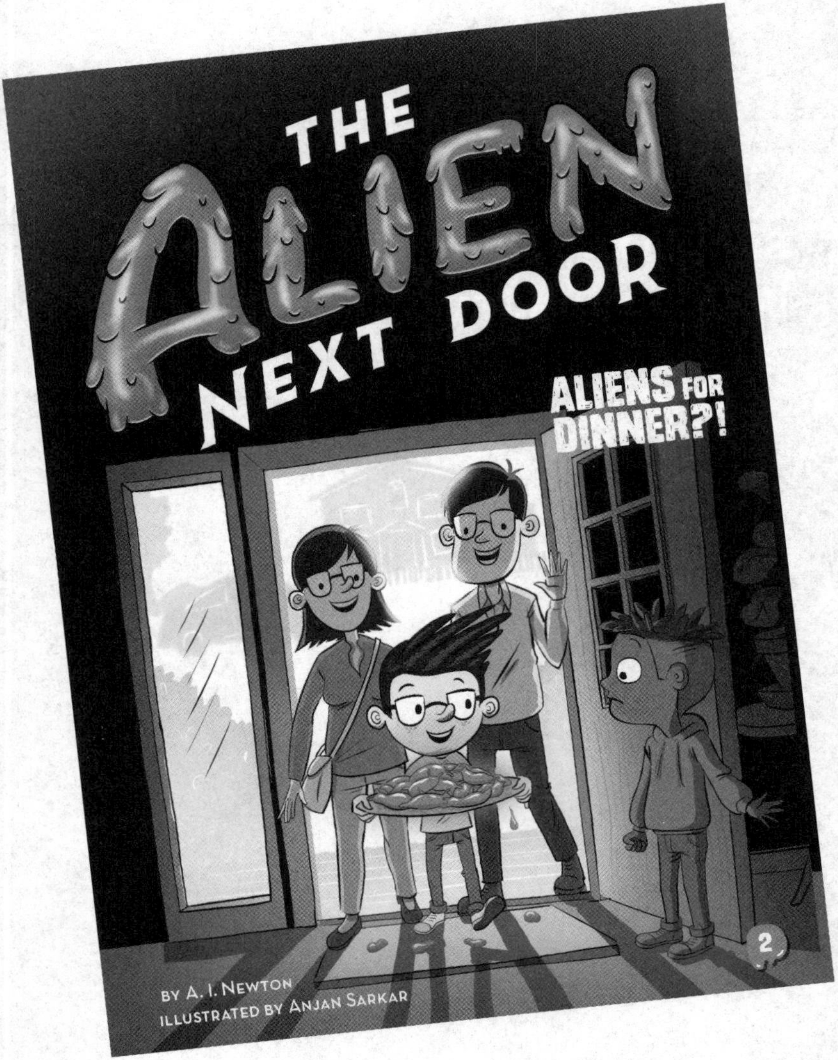
THE ALIEN NEXT DOOR
ALIENS FOR DINNER?!
2
BY A. I. NEWTON
ILLUSTRATED BY ANJAN SARKAR

HARRIS WALKER RAN OUT onto the Jefferson Elementary School soccer field. It was Friday afternoon, and practice was about to begin.

Harris's best friend, Roxy Martinez, trotted up next to him.

"It was fun having Zeke over last weekend, right? I hope you're done with that 'Zeke is an alien' nonsense," she said.

Zeke was Harris's new next-door

neighbor. He had only been at their school for a couple of weeks.

But Harris believed that Zeke was an alien—a real-life alien who somehow came here from another planet. Harris saw Zeke do things that would be impossible for any human kid to do, like move things with his mind, make rainbows suddenly appear in the science lab, and even balance on his fingertips.

"I did have fun. Zeke's a nice kid," Harris replied.

But I still think he's an alien, Harris thought.

Coach Ruffins blew his whistle.

"Okay, everyone, let's get this practice going!" he shouted.

Harris, Roxy, and the rest of the players spent the next hour working on passing, shooting, and defense.

When the practice was nearly over, Harris saw Zeke walking onto the field. A soccer ball flew right toward the front of Zeke's head.

"Look out!" Harris shouted.

He watched in amazement as the ball changed direction, all by itself. It swung around Zeke's head and continued into the goal.

Harris turned to Roxy.

"Did you see that?!" he asked her, sure that she must have seen Zeke control the ball with his mind.

"Yeah," said Roxy, "the ball came so close to hitting Zeke's head! I'm glad he didn't get hurt."

Drats! Harris thought. *From her angle, it must have looked normal.*

"What's up, Zeke?" Harris asked casually as the three friends walked back toward the school.

"I just wanted to thank you again for a great time hanging out at your house, Harris," said Zeke. "And also to invite the both of you to my house tomorrow. We could hang out and play. And my parents are anxious to meet you."

"Sounds great!" said Roxy. She looked at Harris, waiting for him to accept, too.

This is the perfect opportunity to research Zeke's alien family, Harris thought. *I can finally find out what's behind those dark curtains and prove once and for all that he's an alien!*

"I'd love to come over, Zeke," Harris said, giving Roxy a look that said: *See? I don't think he's an alien anymore.*

"Great!" said Zeke. "See you tomorrow!"

A. I. NEWTON always wanted to travel into space, visit another planet, and meet an alien. When that didn't work out, he decided to do the next best thing—write stories about aliens! The Alien Next Door series gives him a chance to imagine what it's like to hang out with an alien. And you can do the same—unless you're lucky enough to live next door to a real-life alien!

ANJAN SARKAR graduated from Manchester Metropolitan University with a degree in illustration. He worked as an illustrator and graphic designer before becoming a freelancer, where he now gets to work on all sorts of different illustration projects! He lives in Sheffield, England.

anjansarkar.co.uk

LOOK FOR MORE BOOKS IN
THE *ALIEN NEXT DOOR* SERIES!

Journey to some magical places, rock out, and find your inner superhero with these other chapter book series from **Little Bee Books**!

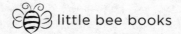

little bee books